# JOHN
# HAN
## INDEPENDENT BOY

Written by
## *Kathryn Cleven Sisson*

Illustrated by
## Cathy Morrison

Patria Press, Inc.
PO Box 752
Carmel IN  46082
www.patriapress.com

Printed and bound in the United States of America
10  9  8  7  6  5  4  3  2  1

Text originally published by the Bobbs-Merrill Company, 1963, in the Childhood
of Famous Americans Series®. The Childhood of Famous Americans Series® is a
registered trademark of Simon & Schuster, Inc.

Library of Congress Cataloging-in-Publication Data

Sisson, Kathryn Cleven, 1904-
    John Hancock : independent boy / by Kathryn Cleven Sisson ; illustrated by
Cathy Morrison.
    p. cm. — (Young patriots series ; v. 9)
    "Originally published by the Bobbs-Merrill Company in the Childhood of
Famous American Series, 1963"—Copyright page.
    ISBN 1-882859-45-6 (hardcover) — ISBN 1-882859-46-4 (pbk.) 1. United
States. Declaration of Independence—Signers—Biography—Juvenile
literature. 2. Hancock, John, 1737-1793—Childhood and youth—Juvenile
literature. 3. Statesmen—United States—Biography—Juvenile literature. I.
Morrison, Cathy, ill. II. Title. III. Series.

E302.6.H23S57 2004
973.3'092—dc22                                              2004001507

Edited by Harold Underdown
Design by inari

# Contents

# Illustrations

*Dedication*

*To my granddaughter*

*Lori Kay*

## Publishers Note

In John Hancock's time, native Americans were referred
to as "Indians." We realize the term is no longer in
general use today, but in the interest of staying historically
accurate we have kept it in the text.

# Books in the Young Patriots Series

Watch for more **Young Patriots** Coming Soon
Visit www.patriapress.com for updates!

# Chapter 1

# Johnny Meets Little Turtle

Johnny Hancock knelt under the lilac bush. He peeked out at the black dragon coming toward him. Then he looked at his sister Mary's wooden doll, lying in the dirt."Fear not, fair one," he said. "Saint George will save you."

He lifted his long stick. A cold drop of rain from the lilac leaves ran down his cheek.

The black dragon snorted and came closer to the garden.

The lilac bush stood behind Parson John Hancock's square white house in Braintree, in the royal colony of Massachusetts. Hancocks had lived near Boston, for a hundred years. Now it was the summer of 1742.

The black dragon was old Dame Clark's black pig, Daisy. Daisy was always getting loose. Then she would dig up the neighbors' gardens.

"You won't dig up our garden," five-year-old Johnny shouted. He ran toward the black pig, shaking his stick.

Daisy squealed, "Oink, oink," but she didn't run away. Instead, she ran right at Johnny. Before he could say "scat!" she dodged his stick and ran between his legs.

Johnny felt himself being lifted up. Suddenly he was riding on Daisy's slippery back. He started to slide off and he grabbed for her curly tail.

Then he bounced off and rolled into a puddle left from the rain. Daisy ran squealing around the house. Someone else would have to catch her. Suddenly Johnny heard someone laughing behind him.

"Ho, ho! Ha, ha!"

Then his friend John Adams came running up. John, who was past six, was short and sturdy. Johnny called him "Jay."

"That looked so funny," Jay said with a grin. He

put down the basket he carried.

Johnny scrambled to his feet. The back of his dress was wet. Johnny had to wear a dress until he went to school, like all small boys did.

"Let's see," Jay Adams said. He pulled Johnny around. "You'll be in trouble."

"I will not," Johnny said. "I have lots of clothes." His dark eyes flashed, but he and his friend both knew that a parson's son didn't have many clothes.

"Johnny! Johnny Hancock!" Mary Hancock stepped out of the kitchen door. There was a smear of corn meal on her cheek. She was only two years older than Johnny, but she often helped their Mother.

"What have you done to your nice dress? Oh, Mother-r-r!" she called.

"Aw-w-w, I fell. The dragon knocked me over. Do you have to tell Mother?"

Mary frowned and gave him a gentle shove toward the kitchen door. Then she remembered her manners. "Will you come, too, Jay?"

"No, thank you, Mary," Jay said. "I have to go to the mill and then back home. I stopped to tell Johnny I can go fishing with him tomorrow. There's no school."

The Adams family lived on a farm at the foot of Penn's Hill. It was about a mile down the Coast

Road which wound along Boston Bay. From the top of Penn's Hill one could see ten miles across Boston Bay to Boston Town itself.

Jay Adams picked up his basket of corn. He ran around the house to the road. Johnny followed his sister slowly into the kitchen. Mother glanced up from the fireplace. Her face looked warm under her frilled white cap. Mary turned Johnny around so that Mother could see his back. "He's all wet."

Mother stood up. She smoothed down the blue apron she wore over her blue and white striped skirt. "Maybe I should let you wash your own clothes. Then you might learn to stay clean."

"Yes, Mother."

"Go to your room and find a fresh dress," she said. "I am much too busy. A neighbor just brought me word from Boston Town. Your Uncle Thomas Hancock and Aunt Lydia are coming here to visit tomorrow."

"Uncle Tom!" Johnny clapped his hands. "Now I can ride in the carriage!"

"Mother," Mary said, "I think Johnny likes fine things too well. Doesn't Father say that is a sin?"

"That's what the old Puritans believed. But people are earning more than in the old days."

"Uncle Thomas has a fine house in Boston. He must have—" Mary began.

Mother frowned. "Yes, your father's brother is very rich. He is a merchant and a trader with England. He has worked very hard. It is too bad he has no children."

Baby Ebenezer started to cry. He was learning to walk and had just taken a tumble in a corner of the kitchen.

"Oh, dear," said Mother. "Will you quiet him, Mary? Your father is working on his two Sunday sermons, and I must get my bread baked. If I'd only known Thomas and Lydia were coming I might have sent to Boston for wheat flour."

Johnny ran out of the room. When he came back in dry clothes he asked Mother, "When will they get here? I can't wait."

"I'll tell you about it at supper, son. We shall eat as soon as Father finishes his sermons. Now run along and don't bother me."

Johnny gave a sigh. "That will be a long time," he said. He went out to the barn to pet Father's horse, Betsy.

Johnny was eating breakfast early the next morning when he heard Jay Adams' whistle outside. The family ate often in the big kitchen, a room added on to the back of the house.

Johnny looked at Father.

"Wait until we say the prayer, John." Father smiled kindly at him.

Johnny had often heard people say that Parson Hancock was wise, kind, and a very good speaker. He knew that people came from far away to hear him preach.

When Johnny at last ran to the door, he saw his friend Jay waiting with a fishing pole over his shoulder.

"Good morrow to you," Johnny said. "Do you have a pole for me?"

"No, I'll cut you one from a young tree with my pocketknife," Jay told him. "I have a fish hook for you, though."

Mother went to the door. "Watch him well, Jay. Stay on the bridge to fish. I don't want him falling into the creek."

"Yes, ma'am."

"And be back for dinner this noon, Johnny. Today is Saturday. Your uncle and aunt will come this afternoon. Good-by, boys."

Johnny tried hard to keep up with Jay Adams' trot. They went up the dusty highway past a few scattered houses and some orchards to Black Creek. The creek flowed into Boston Bay.

When the boys reached the log bridge that

crossed the creek, they were warm from the August sun. Jay put one of the worms he had brought with him on his hook. He gave his pole to Johnny to hold. Johnny dropped the hook and line into the water.

Then Jay found a long green stick on the creek bank and cut it with his knife. He tied a line and hook to it for Johnny.

The two boys fished and fished, but they didn't get a bite. Some dark clouds started to move across the sky.

"If I could just get one fish for my uncle and aunt," Johnny thought. "Everyone eats fish on Saturdays. And I'll have to go home soon."

Just then he looked up. He saw a head peek out from behind a tree. It was a boy with bright black eyes and long black hair.

Johnny gave Jay's foot a little kick. "Look!"

Jay's round face broke into a smile.

"Well! It's Little Turtle. He's one of the Ponkapoag Indians. They're camping at Colonel Quincy's farm near the bay. They have to live on a place at Stoughton, but they come here each year for the fishing."

Now the Indian boy was standing at the end of the bridge. "Fish?" he asked. "How many?"

Jay made a face. "Not one, Little Turtle."

Little Turtle edged closer. "I catch."

"Go ahead."

"I get fish—you give hook?"

"Yes," Johnny whispered eagerly to Jay. "Give him my hook."

Jay nodded. "Show us, Little Turtle."

Little Turtle rubbed his bare toes over the logs of the bridge. A slow smile spread across his face.

He pointed to a shiny blue dragonfly that had lighted on the rushing water. *Swish!* Bubbles marked the spot where a fish had snapped up the dragonfly.

"Fish eat flies, grasshoppers today," Little Turtle said. He moved his brown hands like wings. "No worms."

"Grasshoppers! We'll catch some!" Johnny and Jay cried in the same breath.

Together the three boys roamed the creek banks. The sun went under a cloud, and they heard the rumble of summer thunder.

Soon each boy had a grasshopper in his closed fist. Little Turtle put a grasshopper on Johnny's hook and handed the pole to Johnny. Jay put one on his hook.

Johnny's grasshopper had floated downstream only a moment or two when Johnny felt a sudden tug. The grasshopper disappeared, and the pole pulled at Johnny's hand as if it were alive.

"I got one!" he shouted. "What'll I do?"

"Hang on!" Jay shouted. "I have one, too."

Johnny pulled and pulled. Would his green stick hold? It did not look strong.

Little Turtle put his hands on the stick. Together he and Johnny gave a great jerk. The fish flew out of the creek.

Jay flipped his fish out of the water, too. "Oh, did you ever see such a big one?" Johnny said excitedly. He dragged his gasping prize over beside Jay's fish.

"Mine's larger," Jay declared after measuring the two fish carefully. "But yours is good for your first fish."

Suddenly rain started to fall. "Oh, we've got to go!" Jay said. "Under those trees until it stops raining."

"Tree no good in bad storm," Little Turtle spoke up. "Lightning hit. Come. Go wigwam."

Jay grabbed Johnny's hand. "Let's go," he said. "Hurry!"

They followed the Indian boy along the creek bank. Johnny's short legs had trouble keeping up with the older boys. His bare feet slipped on a muddy spot, and he fell to his knees. He brushed the rain out of his eyes.

He was glad, indeed, to crowd into Little Turtle's wigwam. It was placed with several others among some pine trees. Fish nets were spread over low bushes near by. The fish that had been spread out to dry on trays and sticks were now covered with pieces of old canvas.

Inside the wigwam it was dark and smoky. An opening at the top let out the smoke from the tiny cook fire. A wet, thin dog smelling of fish steamed close to the fire.

Little Turtle's father, White Bear, sat cross-legged on the dirt floor. People gave him the English name of Moses and called him "King" because he was the last head of the small tribe.

Little Turtle spoke to his family in strange words. Then White Bear spoke. "Welcome to our wigwam, young braves."

"Thank you," the boys murmured and sat down on the ground.

Little Turtle's mother brought blackberries in a polished bowl made from a knot of maple wood. Johnny knew his mother prized one like it very highly.

Johnny stuffed the berries in his mouth.

White Bear spoke again. "We come here to catch fish and dry them. In winter we have only dried fish to eat. Now the Quincy family shares its fruit and cider with us. We share with you."

Johnny was sorry he had eaten the food. He sat and listened to the rain outside. Dogs and children were noisy in the next wigwam.

Little Turtle's mother brought blackberries in a polished bowl made from maple wood.

Johnny felt hot and sticky in his damp clothes. He wanted to go home with his prize. He patted the dead fish, which was still fastened to the hook and line.

"Here's the hook we promised you," he said suddenly. He handed the fish over to Little Turtle, who easily took out the hook.

The rain stopped. Little Turtle went outside. In a moment be was back with a handful of long wet grass from the creek bank. He wrapped it around Johnny's fish and handed it back to him with a shy smile. Then he did the same for Jay.

Johnny and Jay looked outside. Sunlight danced through the wet pine branches and across the golden grain fields stretching down to the sea. The air grew hot again.

"Good-by and thanks!" Jay said to their Indian friends.

Johnny said, "I'll bring you some eggs."

As they ran back to the main road, the long grass whipped water over their bare legs.

When Johnny entered the kitchen, he heard a fish peddler's horn sounding down the road.

Sister Mary spied his fish. "Oh, you really caught one! See, Mother, isn't it fine?"

Mother already was broiling several of the peddler's fat codfish in a long-handled iron frying pan.

"Where have you been, Johnny? We were worried during the shower. I see you're muddy again."

"But look at my fish! Mother, I prom—"

"Aye, you've done well." She patted his head. "Give it to me and I shall clean it outside. Mary, hold the pan over the fire. Mind, don't burn your fingers."

He was the first one of the family to see the open carriage with two horses as it pulled up before the gate. In it sat stout Uncle Thomas in his large powdered wig. Across from him spread Aunt Lydia, a mountain of a woman.

She stopped at the door. "Change to a clean dress, Johnny, and put on your shoes. You know Uncle Thomas and Aunt Lydia are coming."

Uncle Thomas! Johnny stood still. He had forgotten in his excitement over the fish. He was the first one of the family to see the open carriage with two horses as it pulled up before the gate. In it sat stout Uncle Thomas in his large powdered wig. Across from him spread Aunt Lydia, a mountain of a woman.

Prince, the coachman, jumped down. He and Uncle Thomas helped Aunt Lydia unfold from the carriage and step down to the ground.

Aunt Lydia's eyes were black and shiny as beetles. She had stern eyebrows. But Johnny was not afraid of her. He knew she loved him.

Uncle Tom, who looked splendid in blue silk and gold lace, lifted Johnny high in the air. He rode him on his broad shoulder into the house.

"Heh, heh!" he chuckled. "What a fine lad! Could be a mite heavier, though. Just come to Boston to visit us, my boy, and we'll fatten you up."

Mother took them into the cool parlor. Here she had her best silver candlesticks and chairs with seats of red velvet.

Aunt Lydia's chair squeaked when she let herself down into it. She and her wide skirts of soft Chinese cotton hid the entire chair. Johnny thought she looked as if she were sitting on nothing at all!

"Yes, indeed," she was saying. "We've come to hear one of your sermons tomorrow, Pastor John. See that it's a good one."

"I do my best, Lydia." Father smiled, not minding a bit. "And how is your shipping business in Boston Town, Tom?" He turned to his younger brother.

"Business is fine!" Uncle Tom replied with a chuckle. "But only because I was smart enough to lay in a large supply of whale oil before this war started in Europe. There's a big market for whale oil in England."

Then he frowned. "If only England would let us trade wherever we wanted to, instead of only with her. But we have ways of getting around that sometimes."

Parson Hancock said, "We must guard our rights as free Englishmen, Thomas. Our royal Massachusetts charter gives us great freedom—more than we had in England. And we must keep it so."

Johnny didn't know what all this meant. But he knew better than to speak when grown-ups were talking.

He tugged at Uncle Tom's arm. At last his uncle looked down at him with a smile. "Eh?"

"If you please, sir—" Johnny waved his hand toward the window. The carriage horses were still standing outside, tied to the hitching post in front of the house.

"Ah, you remember I promised you a ride the last time I came, do you? A ride you shall have, just as soon as the horses are rested a bit. They pulled quite a load from Boston Town." He laughed, and Aunt Lydia frowned.

Later, when Johnny, Mary, and Uncle Tom were going out the door, Johnny suddenly stopped. He didn't know what to say.

"My promise!" he thought. "I told the Indians I'd

bring them eggs and I forgot!"

"I can't go," he said fiercely. He ran back to Mother and whispered in her ear. "May I borrow eggs to give to the Indians out at the Quincy farm? They gave me fruit when they took me in from the rain. I promised."

Mother smiled down at him with a shake of her head. "What shall I do with you, Johnny Hancock? You're like all the Hancocks, always giving. Yes, take that small basket of eggs out of the pantry. A neighbor brought us an extra dozen this morning."

Besides the money Braintree paid Parson Hancock, the villagers often brought the family food. "Country pay," it was called.

"Thank you, Mother," Johnny said. He got the eggs. Then Uncle Tom popped his head into the kitchen to see what Johnny was doing.

"So you want to walk way out to the Indian camp instead of riding with me, heh?"

"I-I want to go, Uncle, but I promised, and-and you said you would drive south on the road to Plymouth."

"You're a good boy, Johnny," Uncle Tom said. "I think Prince can turn the horses around the other way. We can drive out to the camp to deliver your eggs."

And so they did.

# Chapter 2

# Up to Boston Town

A cold March wind whistled around Johnny's knit cap. He clutched his father's black cloak tightly as they rode through the snow on Betsy, the family horse.

They came to a small schoolhouse sitting under a big tree. "Whoa, Betsy," Father said.

"Thank you, Father!" Johnny slipped down from the horse. "That was better than walking over a mile through the snowdrifts."

"You'll have to walk home at four o'clock, Johnny. I have a long ride to visit sick folk and make calls. I won't come back this way."

"Yes, sir." Johnny looked down the road at the Adams farmhouse. He saw no sign of his friend Jay. It wasn't eight o'clock yet, when Dame School started on winter mornings.

Inside, the school room was cold. Several of the

older boys were trying to build up the fire. Their breaths steamed in the cold air.

Dame Belcher, the teacher, sat holding her fingers to the fire. A piece of sewing lay in her lap. She looked like a plump brown hen with a big white cap tied under its chin.

Johnny kept on his coat and mittens. He bowed to Dame Belcher and said, "Good morrow, Mistress." Then he sat down on a form, a plank or wooden bench.

He took off the hornbook that hung around his neck. This hornbook was a piece of wood shaped like a paddle. A piece of paper about three by four inches square was fastened to it. The letters of the alphabet, a verse, and the Lord's Prayer were printed on it. A thin sheet of horn, through which he could read the letters, covered the paper. All children learned their letters from the horn book.

Sister Mary had given Johnny hers. Now that she was eight, she would no longer go to Dame School. Father planned to teach her at home.

Johnny opened the copybook he had made by folding sheets of large brown paper together. He took out his lead plummet, the small stick of lead which he used to write. He began to print his name carefully in his copybook.

School was still new to him, for he had just been

going since his sixth birthday in January. After the morning prayer, Dame Belcher asked Jay Adams to pass out fresh goose quills. She mixed ink powder and water for the ink pots.

Johnny scratched out his name on the paper with his quill pen. He wished the ink wouldn't spatter so much. "But you can really tell what the letters are," he thought.

He showed his copybook to Will Salter, who sat next to him. Will looked and snickered.

"What's wrong? Can't you read it?" Johnny whispered crossly.

Will put his hand over his mouth and laughed. "Just about. The letters are crooked and there's a blot—"

"Will Salter!" Dame Belcher stood before the boys. She gave Will a sharp rap on the head with her thimble. "Put on the dunce cap and stand in the corner for laughing and whispering."

Will hung his head and slowly went to the corner of the room.

"You will go there, too, John Hancock, if you whisper more." She looked at his copybook. "Humph! A parson's son must do better. Keep working, young man."

"Yes, mistress," Johnny said, his face hot. He looked back to where Jay Adams sat with the older boys. They were reading their New England Primers. Jay grinned and winked.

Johnny forgot his troubles with writing when he finally reached home at dusk. The race home from school and a rousing snowball attack on Daisy, the roaming black pig, had warmed him in the chill air.

He burst into the kitchen. "I'm home!" he called out. The good smell of an Indian pudding of corn meal and molasses cooking made him hungry. The pudding was boiling in a copper kettle that hung from a pothook over the fire in the big fireplace.

Father rested with his boots off before the blazing fire. He was reading a letter aloud to Mother. She held two-year-old Ebenezer in her lap. Mary was knitting a long wool stocking.

Mother looked up and smiled. "Welcome, son. A letter for Father was waiting at the tavern. It's from Uncle Tom. His gout, his sore foot, still keeps him from paying us a visit."

"Oh, I'm sorry!" Johnny was disappointed.

"He says the road will soon be cleared by the farmers' ox teams. The weather is sure to turn better. He wants us to come in to Boston."

"Huzzah!" Johnny shouted and jumped for joy.

Father shook his head. "Little Ebenezer's cough is bad, and I feel unwell tonight, son. We must put it off."

"It's only ten miles or so, Father," Mary dared to say.

Johnny held his breath. Father looked stern and said, "Mary! We shall wait."

A month later Johnny and Mary rode through Boston's arched brick gates on Boston Neck. The town was almost surrounded by water. A mile of narrow mudflats, called the Neck, tied it to the mainland.

On one side Johnny looked out over wide Boston Harbor, spotted with islands and the Castle Island Fort. On the other side he saw the Charles River flowing down to the harbor.

Uncle Tom's carriage rolled up Cornhill Street. Here the houses stood close together. The horses' hoofs struck the cobblestones sharply as the carriage passed rattling carts and people hurrying to and fro.

This was not Johnny's first visit to the great Hancock house on Beacon Hill. But he did not remember the house clearly from earlier visits.

"Isn't it exciting to travel alone, John?" Mary laughed and squeezed his hand. Father still was not well, and Mother wouldn't leave him. She had let the children come alone.

"Yes," Johnny nodded, with one hand on his new three-cornered hat.

Prince, the coachman, turned the carriage west up Beacon Street to Beacon Hill, the highest of Boston's three hills. The street ran along a wide green field in which cows were grazing.

"That's Boston Common," Mary cried. The Common's forty acres stretched down to the banks of the Charles River.

Just then Johnny saw Uncle Tom's house. "There it is! Isn't it fine?" he said. A fence on a low stone wall ran in front of the stone mansion.

Prince stopped the carriage. Johnny jumped out and ran up the tree-bordered walk. He banged on the brass door knocker until a servant opened the wide doors. And there stood Uncle Tom and Aunt Lydia in the large central hall. They welcomed the children with a hug.

"I've stayed home from my 'counting-room' and store this morning to wait for you young ones," Uncle Tom said with a big smile.

Servants took the children's boxes up to separate guest rooms, for they were to stay two weeks in Boston.

"We've waited dinner for you," Aunt Lydia said. She led the way into the dining room. Servants seated them at a large mahogany table. There were forks for everyone, and dishes of rare china as well as the usual pewter.

Uncle Tom urged Johnny to eat more of the fresh roast meat, the chicken pies, and jellies. His face grew redder and redder as he ate his meal and drank from his silver tankard. "Eat well and you'll be strong," he declared.

When he left in his carriage he said, "Tomorrow you and Mary shall visit the zoo at the docks. There are other surprises there for good boys and girls." He winked and chuckled.

Johnny had never seen a zoo. "Is it like Noah's Ark in my primer?" he asked.

"Goodness, no! It's better than pictures." His aunt's eyebrows went up and her black eyes smiled at him. "Wait and see."

Johnny thought he couldn't wait, but he slept soundly in his deep feather bed after all. Morning came before he knew it.

When he saw the waterfront the next day, Johnny thought it was wonderful. He loved the smell of the sea, of fresh and dried fish, and of tarred rope that hung over the busy seaport. The closer the carriage came to the wharfs edging the shore, the stronger the smell grew.

Mary held her nose with her small gloved fingers. "Braintree smells better," she said.

Prince pulled in the horses at the head of Long Wharf. The town's largest wharf stretched from

busy King Street a half-mile out into the harbor.
Warehouses, stores, and fish markets were built on
one side of the wharf. Large ships tied up on the
other side.

Johnny stared at strange sailors in belled blue
trousers and tarred pigtails. Sea captains, clerks
with ledgers, fish peddlers with tin horns or bells

Mary held her nose with her small gloved fingers.
"Braintree smells better," she said.

crowded and pushed.

"Oys! Buy any oys?" an oysterman called. He carried his wares in a sack on his back.

Hay wagons and two-wheeled carts loaded with firewood rumbled back and forth all day, Uncle Thomas said. But even above Boston's noise, Johnny could hear the cries of swooping gulls and the beat of the sea.

Uncle Thomas stopped at a wooden shed on the wharf. Inside a wooden cage in the shed sat a large white bear.

"O-o-oh!" Johnny gasped. "What kind is it? I thought bears were brown or black."

"This is a polar bear. It lives far north where the land is always white with snow."

The children laughed at the tricks of a dancing dog brought from Europe. They saw bright birds and a chattering brown monkey, too. But they turned quickly away from the sight of a pirate's head pickled in a jar.

"Now it's time for the big surprise," Uncle Tom declared. He waved his gold-headed cane toward the next largest wharf two blocks away. "It's near Clark's Wharf. We shall walk."

Johnny and Mary thought it was fun to stare into the tiny shop windows as they walked up Anne Street into Fish Street. A leather shop, a chemist's, a baker's, and a sail-maker's all slowed their steps.

"Here is the Revere silver shop," Uncle Tom said as they passed on. "I do business with silversmith Revere. Here we are!" He stopped in front of a shop. "It's Mr. Fletcher's store."

They stepped inside. It looked like other stores

to Johnny. Imported cloth, candlesticks, tea, paper, and hardware were laid out on shelves. Uncle Tom led the way to a door in the back. A clerk came up to them.

"We wish to see the town," Uncle Tom said. "That will be four shillings, six pence." The clerk took the coins with a smile.

Johnny and Mary looked at each other in surprise. What could cost so much to see?

Spread out on a wide table was a tiny toy town. "Why, it's Boston Town!" Johnny guessed with a laugh. "See all the church steeples and the docks and ships!"

They heard a whirring noise, and everything started to move. The wheels of the coaches and carts in the narrow streets began to turn. The ships sailed in and out of the harbor. A little powder mill in one corner started working.

Johnny darted from side to side of the busy town in his excitement. "How does it work?"

Mary clapped her hands daintily.

"Heh, heh! Knew you'd like it, lad. Would buy it for you, but old Fletcher won't sell. He says there are twelve hundred gears and wheels making this thing run. Now I have business to attend to. We'll come back again."

"Just a little longer, please, sir?"

"Another time, another time." Before Johnny knew it, he was standing in the cold April sunshine outside the shop.

A handsome young fellow about seventeen walked up to Uncle Tom. "Your pardon, sir. May I speak to you? It's private business."

"Heh? What?" Uncle Tom looked surprised. The boy was dressed plainly and his wavy black hair was tied neatly back of his neck. He wore no hat. "What private business could you have? See my clerk." Uncle Tom started to move on.

"Wait, sir." The young fellow forced a smile. "You know Mr. Gerrish and his book shop?"

"I should. I was apprenticed to his father. I got my start by learning the book-binding business from him."

"True, sir," said the young man.

"As I have just learned it there, I would like to work for you, sir."

"Heh? Why do you not stay with Gerrish?"

"Because, sir, I heard about you often in my seven years. I was bound out to Mr. Gerrish as an apprentice, but I'm free now."

"You're an orphan? English?"

"Irish, begorra! The name's Tim O'Toole, sir. I have a fine tale for the youngsters, if you'll let them listen."

"Do listen, Uncle," Johnny begged. He liked this young man and wanted his Uncle Thomas to hire him.

Uncle Tom waved his cane at Prince, who waited near by with the carriage. "We'll sit in my carriage. You may stand beside it and tell your story, but I promise nothing."

After they had seated themselves, Tim O'Toole said, "You have heard many a sad tale, sadder, maybe, than mine, but I wish no sadder tale on any soul." He gave a great sigh and rolled his dark eyes at Johnny and Mary.

They sighed in return. Their eyes didn't leave his face.

"My mother died in Ireland when I was a lad of ten. My father was a sea captain. Not knowing what to do with me, he took me to sea with him. We sailed for America. On the way over here he died suddenly. The crew buried him at sea." He took a deep breath.

"Go on, go on," ordered Uncle Tom.

"Begorra, sir, that crew—that crew did a terrible thing. The next day a shipload of orphan boys and girls hailed us. These orphans were on their way to be bound out for service in America, the captain of their ship said.

"The crew sold me to that captain of the orphan ship, sir, and he brought me to Boston Town. He bound me out to Samuel Gerrish. There I've worked these seven years."

He stopped, and then rushed on. "I'm a good worker and write a fine hand. My master will have to admit that. Won't you try me, please?"

Johnny held his breath. Uncle Tom looked at him, a slight smile on his lips. Johnny said, "Say yes, please, sir."

"Call at my counting-room tomorrow, O'Toole. Ask for my chief clerk. I'll have him check on you. Maybe he can find a place for you somewhere."

"Thank you, sir." Tim bowed low. "I'll be there early. God bless you all!"

"Good luck, Tim O'Toole," Johnny called.

"A likeable lad," Uncle Tom chuckled. "He can tell a sad tale, can't he?"

"Yes, I like him," Johnny said. "Don't you, Mary? I hope I see him again the next time I come to Boston."

"Maybe that won't be very soon," Mary said with a wise look. "I've had a wonderful time, Uncle Tom, but it's too noisy here in Boston. And smelly, too. I like to live in Braintree best, I think."

"Braintree is dull," Johnny said stoutly. "I wish we could live here. When I grow up I want to be a general or a sea captain and sail the seven seas. Then I can live in Boston when I'm not at sea or fighting a war somewhere."

# Chapter 3

# A New Home and a New Family

Johnny didn't know that his wish would soon come true. A year later, in May, 1744, Father fell ill and died. Everything was mixed up for Johnny after that, until one day Mother called him to her and said sadly, "We can't live here much longer, Johnny. A new parson is coming. He will use this parsonage. I must find another place to live. Your grandfather, Bishop Hancock, says we can live with him in Lexington. But that means more mouths to feed, and he is an old man."

"What will we do then, Mother?" Seven-year-old Johnny looked up at his mother and wondered. "Where will we go?"

Mother took his hand. "Your grandfather, Uncle Thomas, and I have decided what is best. I hope you will think it is, too. I need Mary to help with little

There were new black slippers with silver buckles,
a ruffled shirt, a blue silk coat, and a white waist-coat —
and a small wig.

Ebenezer, and she doesn't care for Boston Town."

Johnny stood quietly and waited.

"Uncle Thomas wants you to live with him. He wants to adopt you and to send you to a grammar school and to Harvard College. I could not do that. Father wanted you to go to college, John, as he did."

Johnny nodded and swallowed a lump in his throat. "I know."

"Will you go to Uncle Tom's?"

"Yes, Mother, if I have to. I would like to live with him." He didn't look at her.

Mother gave him a hug. "We will miss you, son, but will try to see you often. You will have a fine future with Uncle Tom."

Johnny buried his head on Mother's shoulder so she wouldn't see his tears.

The next morning Uncle Thomas arrived. He brought a box of fine clothes for Johnny. There were new black slippers with silver buckles, a ruffled shirt, a blue silk coat, and a white waist-coat—and a small wig.

Johnny threw the white wig in a corner. "I won't wear it," he said with spirit.

Mother and Uncle Tom smiled. "That was your aunt's idea," Uncle said, "just to try it out. You'd have to have your head shaved first, you know, Johnny."

"No, sir!" Johnny clutched his brown hair tied neatly behind his neck. "I'll keep my own, thank you."

A short time later Johnny was sitting stiffly in his new clothes in Uncle Tom's carriage, ready to go to Boston.

"Good-by, good-by, and God bless you," Mother and Mary said to him. Little Ebenezer laughed and said, "Bye-bye."

Jay Adams stood waving at the gate, too. He had come over from the Latin School near the Meeting House to see Johnny off.

As Prince drove away, an old black pig ran squealing from in front of the horses' hoofs. Two white piglets followed her.

"It's Daisy!" Johnny said, and even felt sorry to leave her.

Uncle Tom looked down at Johnny. "Boston is not far away," he said. "Your mother and Mary and Ebenezer will come to visit us."

Johnny nodded. "May Jay Adams visit me?"

"Of course, my boy."

Johnny began to feel better and enjoy the ride to Boston.

"Here we are!" Uncle Tom said when they drew up before his fine mansion. He and Johnny got out and Prince drove the carriage into the coach house on the left side of the house.

Aunt Lydia met Johnny in the wide hall with its curving staircase. "Welcome to your new home, dear Johnny," she said.

"Thank you, Aunt Lydia." Johnny swept off his three-cornered hat and made a bow as Mother had taught him. Then he was caught up in Aunt Lydia's arms.

"Here, here" and "Heh, heh," said Uncle Tom. He patted them both on the back.

Aunt Lydia let Johnny go, to his relief. She stood back to see his new clothes. "Now you are dressed as the son of a Boston merchant should be dressed," she said with a nod. "I see you didn't wear the wig I sent along."

Johnny turned pink. "I like the clothes, and I thank you for them," he said politely. "But the wig—it scratched and was too hot."

His aunt didn't smile. "Well, you shall get used to it some day. Right now you don't need to wear it. Tomorrow we'll go shopping for more clothes. Then we shall see about Latin School."

School had to wait, however. Johnny fell ill and was unable to go. When his fever left him and he was better, a private teacher came to the house. The tutor helped Johnny to learn Latin.

He needed to know Latin because the grammar

schools, the elementary schools of those days, spent most of their time on the study of Latin and Greek.

Behind Uncle Tom's house a large garden swept up Beacon Hill. Johnny liked to sit and study there in the summer house.

When he tired of studying, he would drop *Cheever's Latin Grammar* in his lap and stare at the tar-barrel beacon at the top of the hill. It was fastened to a tall mast.

He would imagine that he was the person chosen to climb the mast and set the beacon alight. Its soaring flames would warn all the countryside around of enemy attack.

Or he could watch the white wings of ships skim across wide, blue Boston Bay. To the north he could look across the Charles River to Cambridge and Harvard College. To the south he could see the rugged blue hills of Dorchester and Braintree.

One afternoon Aunt Lydia came out to the summer house. She wore a high bonnet and a shawl, although it was a warm July day. "Come Johnny. We're going to call on the Quincys this afternoon," she said.

"In Braintree, ma'am?" Johnny's heart beat faster. He jumped to his feet.

His aunt smiled. "No, these Quincys live here in Boston, although they used to live in Braintree. The family is so large it is no wonder you mix them up. We are going to the Edmund Quincys. They have so many children I've lost count of them. Colonel Josiah Quincy's family will be there, too."

Children romped all over the Quincy's' big house on Star Lane, Johnny found out. He met Ned, Sam, Hannah, Jacob, Esther, and more. He gave up trying to sort them out.

The boys played "Scotch-hoppers" and "bat-and-ball" in the cobbled stable-yard beside the house. They played Indian with bows and arrows. They chased the girls around the mulberry tree in the garden.

For this they were roundly scolded. The girls in their long, heavy skirts and cloth shoes could hardly run.

"We'll come over to your house during August vacation," Sam Quincy told Johnny. He was seven years old, too. "We can fly our kites on Boston Common."

And so they did. Johnny was happy to find new friends. "What fun to belong to a large family!" he said.

Uncle Tom took pains to be kind to him.

One noon at dinner he said, "Johnny, I'm not going back to my counting-room this afternoon. I'm taking you down to watch a ship unload. I own part of the goods it brought. I'm lucky it came through safely."

He looked at his wife. "This new war with France and Spain brings us war orders from England. That means we're paid in silver and gold. You know how scarce they are!"

Uncle Tom shook his head with its large white wig. "These sea captains and their sailors have their silver coins melted down and made into bowls and tankards. That makes silver money scarce again! Revere, the silversmith, tells me he keeps very busy."

"Oh, that reminds me," said Aunt Lydia. "Will you stop by Revere's shop and order me a new copper kettle?"

"Yes, my dear." After the prayer, Uncle Tom rose from the table. "Come along, Johnny, my boy. Let us be going."

"Right away, sir. Good-by, Aunt Lydia." Johnny made a bow.

He and Uncle Tom drove down Beacon Hill and soon turned into wide King Street.

"How is Tim O'Toole doing, sir?" Johnny asked. "I would like to see him."

"We'll stop on our way back," Uncle Tom promised. "He's doing very well, very well as a clerk. Writes a fine hand. Even has been made a sergeant in the militia. Started as a drummer boy, you know."

The carriage stopped at the head of Clark's Wharf in Fish Street. Uncle Tom sent Prince off with it to a nearby stable.

Uncle Tom had a warehouse that was built right on the wharf. Here he stored the whale oil and ships' masts that he sent to England. Here, too, he stored the goods that he brought in from the West Indies, England, and Holland—rolls of cloth, nails, hinges, bolts, tools, and tea.

Johnny stood in front of a shop window that faced the busy wharf. A signboard swung over the shop door. On it were painted the words, "Revere, Silversmith."

Just then a husky boy dashed out the door. He carried a basket over his arm. He wore the full leather breeches of Boston apprentice boys and a leather apron.

He bumped square into Johnny and almost knocked him off his feet. "Hey, take care!" Johnny cried angrily.

The brown-haired boy stopped. He nodded quickly to Uncle Tom. "A good morrow to you, Mr. Hancock. I'm Paul, the oldest Revere boy." His brown eyes flickered over at Johnny. "My pardon," he added smiling, "but little fellows should look sharp."

Then with a hearty laugh he ran on."I'll trip, him the next time I see him," Johnny grumbled.

He bumped square into Johnny and almost knocked him off his feet. "Hey, take care!" Johnny cried angrily.

"He's not so much bigger than I am."

"Heh, heh. Don't fret about him. Come along now and watch this brig unload."

The high ship pressed close against the wharf. Cranes creaked as they swung boxes and barrels onto the broad wharf. The captain stood on deck and shouted orders to the dock workers.

Johnny watched, his eyes shining with excitement. He saw dozens of fishing boats and bigger ships tied to the wharfs. He looked up at the forest of wooden roofs and church steeples rising from the shore. And all the while the exciting, shrill, loud noises of the waterfront were in his ears.

He pulled at his uncle's silk coat. "I like all this, Uncle," he said. "I want to be a merchant when I'm a man. I would like to work with you if I may."

Uncle Tom beamed. "Just what I hoped you would say, my lad."

Johnny went on, almost to himself. "Maybe I can be a sea captain or a pirate."

"Ho! Ho!" Uncle Tom's double chins shook. "You'll find pirates enough among our Boston merchants, Johnny!" he said. "Come, let's order the teapot now. Then we can walk back to the 'Bible and Three Crowns.'"

This had been the first of the four shops that Uncle Tom now owned. He had started here as a bookseller.

Then he had gone into the trading business, and now he was the richest man in the Massachusetts Colony.

Almost everything was on sale at Uncle Tom's shop, from things for the home to ships' supplies. The smell of spices, tobacco, and coal dust tickled Johnny's nose when he pushed open the door and went inside.

Uncle Tom's "counting-room" was in the room next to the shop. There the letter-writing of the vast trading business was carried on. Several clerks sat at high desks, pushing goose quill pens across miles of foolscap paper.

"Come, we'll call out young O'Toole," Uncle Tom said.

Johnny followed him happily through the shop and into the counting-room. He was enjoying every moment of this day.

# Chapter 4

# New England Fights the French

The beat of drums and the squeal of fifes awoke Johnny early one morning. He jumped from his high feather bed and rushed to the little balcony over the front door.

Three thousand militiamen were camped on Boston Common. The Royal Governor of Massachusetts had called them up this March of 1745. He planned to attack a French fort in Canada.

"Today's the day!" John, who was now eight, thought excitedly. "The soldiers are going to sail to Nova Scotia and—"

"Johnny!" Aunt Lydia stood behind him. She wore a dressing gown. "Don't stand out here in this damp! You'll catch your death of cold."

Johnny turned to her, almost dancing in his eagerness. "Oh, Aunt! The militiamen are starting.

Hear the drums! Can't we go now?"

"Mercy, it's much too early." Aunt Lydia closed the balcony door and pushed him into his room. "They're not leaving yet."

Johnny put on warm red wool stockings and a wool broadcloth suit. At breakfast he was silent, but he kept his eyes on Uncle Tom.

At last his uncle rose from the table and rubbed his long nose. "Is there a lad here who wants to watch the militia board ship this morning?" he asked.

"Yes, sir, I do!" Johnny grinned happily.

Down at Boston harbor an air of excitement hung over the docks. Sixty ships waited there to take on men and supplies.

A crowd was gathered at Clark's Wharf. Wearing wool cloaks to protect themselves against the sharp ocean wind, Johnny and Uncle Tom mingled with the crowd.

Two merchant friends joined Uncle Tom. They talked about the French fort called Lóuisburg on Cape Breton Island in Canada. "It is a threat to us and our fishing boats. It will be a threat as long as England is at war with France," one merchant said.

The other merchant looked cross. "How can our

militiamen fight real French soldiers? We need men who know how to use big cannon—and how many big cannon do we have?"

"We've taken the cannon from the town's South Battery and from Castle Island Fort in the harbor," Uncle Tom told him. "We've borrowed others from neighboring colonies. I helped find supplies for this adventure. However, we need big guns to storm Fort Louisburg."

"It'll be a miracle if our men capture it," said the merchant. "They will fail."

"Some of the officers know a little gunnery. I have faith in our New England men," Uncle Tom said stoutly.

Johnny nodded proudly. "Even more so," he thought, "since Sergeant Tim O'Toole is going to fight." Where was Tim? Johnny couldn't see him among the line of blue-coated men who were marching aboard the ships at Clark's wharf. Maybe he was at another wharf.

Johnny slipped away through the crowd. He ran along the waterfront, hoping to see Tom. At Long Wharf he saw the *Massachusetts Frigate,* Boston's own warship, tied up alongside the wharf. Militiamen were boarding it, too.

Guns poked their noses out of portholes along its sides. An arm waved from one of the double rows of windows across the ship's stem.

"Johnny Hancock! Oh, Johnny Hancock! Halloo-o-o!"

And there was the black head of Tim O'Toole. Tim grinned and waved his sergeant's cap.

"Good-by, Tim O'Toole," Johnny yelled. He waved as hard as he could. "Good luck! Fight for New England!"

With a last wave, he ran back to seek his uncle. He felt happy to have said good-by to a soldier who was his friend.

Weeks passed by, and all Boston waited for word from Canada. In May a fishing boat brought word that the ships were waiting near Cape Breton Island for the ice to break up in the harbor at Louisburg.

One July night that same year Johnny was deep in dreams. Suddenly the boom of a cannon awoke him. He sat up, his heart thumping. It was almost dawn.

He heard someone gallop up Beacon Hill, shouting, "Fort Louisburg has fallen!" Then church bells began to ring and muskets to fire.

Molly, the Irish maid, came in with a basin of hot water for Johnny to wash in. "Our brave militia

He waved as hard as he could. "Good luck!
Fight for New England!"

has beaten the French soldiers," she said excitedly.

"Huzzah for them!" Johnny shouted. He pranced barefooted about his room.

"It's a great victory for Massachusetts Colony," Uncle Tom declared at breakfast. He helped himself from a silver bowl of hasty pudding that Molly held. "Everyone knows we gave most of the men and ships. And it was the Governor's idea to capture Louisburg."

"To think that Tim O'Toole saw it all!" Johnny burst out. "How soon will he be back?"

"That's hard to say, Johnny. Months, perhaps. Ah, no one will work this happy day!"

Months later, on a cold November day, the first ships came back from Canada. Among them was the *Massachusetts Frigate*.

To Johnny's delight, Jay Adams came to town with his father, Deacon Adams. They went with Johnny and Uncle Tom to see the militia come off the ship.

The tired men marched from Long Wharf up short King Street. They stepped between rows of British soldiers and cadets.

"Huzzah!" Johnny and Jay shouted a welcome along with everyone else.

"Look!" whispered Johnny. "Their red and blue uniforms are all rags."

"Yes, but how proud they look! They know they did a great thing."

"Where's Tim O'Toole?" Johnny hopped from one foot to the other trying to see.

That night every window in the big Hancock house was lighted. Friends had been coming and going all day.

A huge bonfire blazed on the Common across the street. Fireworks banged and rockets glittered overhead. Johnny, Jay, Sam Quincy, and a group of boys sat near the fire, watching. So Johnny was able to see Tim O'Toole clearly when he walked past with a group of soldiers.

"Tim! Sergeant Tim!" Johnny ran and stood in front of the young man.

"Sure, and it's the master's fine boy!" Tim cried. His white teeth flashed and he clapped Johnny on the shoulder.

"How are you? Oh, I'm glad you came by! Please sit here with us and watch the fireworks," Johnny said eagerly. "Then you can tell us all about your taking Fort Louisburg."

"Oh? And is that all you want of me?" Tim asked. But he was kind enough to sit with the boys. He had been sent home early, he said, because he had been ill with camp fever. "Now, then, what do you want to hear first?"

"All of it," Johnny said. "How our militia shot down the high walls of the fort overnight and how—"

"'Twas not that easy, Johnny. First of all, our ships had to meet in Cans Bay. That's five hundred miles north of here. The British finally decided to help and Admiral Warren met us with five warships.

"We had word that the harbor of Louisburg was solid ice. No ships could go in or out, so the French didn't know we were near."

"How near were you?" Johnny put in.

"Only fifty miles away. We waited three weeks. Then, on April 30, we landed half our men in a bay below Fort Louisburg and the other half the next day. The surf was high and the shore rocky, but all our boats landed safely.

"The French fired a signal cannon when they saw our sails. All the people working outside the town rushed inside the walls. A party of French soldiers came out to meet us, but we drove them away.

"We marched over rocks, hills, and through swamps. We made camp two miles from the fort. A big swamp lay between us and the French."

"What did you do then?" Johnny asked.

"We looked up at the thirty-foot-high walls and we wondered how we would ever get in!

"You see, Fort Louisburg sat on the south point of the bay. There was a group of cannon, known as the Grand Battery, in the hills behind the bay. There was also a strong fort on an island in the harbor. We had to take the battery and the island fort as well as the town."

"How did you do it?" Jay Adams asked.

Tom laughed. "Well, my captain, Captain Vaughn, found some naval storehouses in the hills behind the Grand Battery. They held pitch, tar, oil, and gunpowder. We set fire to them. There was a terrible flash when the gunpowder blew up, and clouds of smoke filled the sky."

"The black smoke covered the Grand Battery," Tim went on. "It scared the French soldiers and they ran away. Later, Captain Vaughn sent in an Indian scout to see if all was clear. It was. One of my men (there were thirteen of us) climbed the flagpole and nailed his red coat to it for a flag."

The boys laughed loudly.

"The hardest part was yet to come," Tim told them. "We needed bigger guns to reach the main part of the fort and the island battery. The only heavy guns we had were the ships' guns. We brought them ashore on flatboats. Some were smashed on the rocks by the surf, but we got most of them ashore. Some of us waded in through the icy water carrying powder casks high over our heads.

"Then we pulled the heavy guns on sleds

through the swamp. There were three hundred of us tied to one gun! The guns sank in the mud. All the time we were under fire from the fort.

"One by one, we placed the big guns in the hills overlooking Louisburg. Then, when the guns were ready, we poured cannon fire into the town. We kept at it for a month.

"I fell sick the day the French surrendered. The next day our men marched into the town and the French marched out to sail for France. The day after that it began to rain. It rained for ten days. If the rains had come sooner, we could not have captured Louisburg! Thank the Lord!"

"Nobody can beat our New England men," Johnny said with pride.

Tim laughed, and then coughed. "At least, we know we can lick the French. It's lucky I am I'm here, what with the fever and all. But I'm on the mend, lads. I must go along now."

The boys thanked him for his thrilling story. Now a bright sky rocket streaked like a golden arrow through the blackness overhead.

"We can protect our country ourselves," Johnny thought.

And by his "country" he meant the colony of Massachusetts, not England.

Schoolmaster John Lovely stood over him.

Johnny carefully wiped his quill pen with a bit of cloth. He dipped the point into his inkhorn. Once again he began to copy from his Dilworth speller.

"Master Hancock!" Johnny felt a sharp rap on his hand. "You little wretch!"

He looked up while he rubbed his stinging fingers.

Schoolmaster John Lovely stood over him. He held a ruler in his hand and scowled.

"You've spoiled your paper again," Mr. Lovely scolded. "Hold your pen right, and you won't splash ink on your work. And never use a pen-wiper on a pen!"

Johnny gulped. "But, sir, how do I —"

"See here." The schoolmaster grabbed the pen. He wiped off the pen point with his little finger. Then he pushed back the old powdered wig he wore. He wiped off his finger on the thin strands of gray hair under his wig!

Johnny stared. He tried not to smile, but his teacher's head was dotted with black ink!

"My aunt—" he began to say, then thought better of it. "I'll do better, sir," he promised. He took a fine linen handkerchief from his coat pocket. He wiped his wet hands and then started to work again.

He had gone to South Latin School since he was eight, over a year now. It was on School Street next to King's Chapel and only two blocks from home.

"Will this day never end?" Johnny groaned. How could he think about his bad writing when the French fleet might attack Boston soon?

Only fifteen months before, the New Englanders had taken the great fort of Louisburg. Because of that, the French King was now sending forty warships and a hundred other ships to capture Boston.

A whaling ship and several fishing boats had raced down from the North Atlantic with the news of the mighty French fleet's approach. "They're strung out for miles," the sailors from the boats said. "And they're filled to the masts with French soldiers."

Johnny wondered whether more New England militia had arrived today to camp on the Common's wide green acres. "What a grand sight their tents make!" he thought. "Six thousand men are camped there, ready to fight for Boston and America if need be."

Johnny frowned and bit the end of his quill pen. "I wish Aunt Lydia would let me visit the men in camp," he thought. "But she says they're not Boston men and I shouldn't bother them."

Just this morning she had said, "Thank Heaven, we're safe as long as this south wind keeps blowing." For ten days the wind had come from the south. "The French will have trouble sailing south to Boston against it."

Suddenly the school bell broke into his thoughts. A general prayer was said, and then the boys rushed pell-mell outside.

At once Johnny noticed that the wind had changed. A gusty wind was now coming from the north. It tore showers of October leaves from the trees. And it would speed the French ships toward Boston.

He walked slowly up Beacon Street along one side of the Common. He looked longingly at the bustling camp. Some of his schoolmates were shouting and running toward it.

"If I can't visit the camp, perhaps I can ride over to Sam Quincy's after tea. We can talk about it all. Prince will help me saddle Imp." Johnny loved Imp, his new red-brown pony.

With a last look at the camp, he went up the stone steps of the mansion. Inside, Molly brought Indian pudding and gingerbread on a silver tea tray, while Johnny gave Aunt Lydia a peck on her round cheek.

Uncle Tom came in from his library. There was a worried look on his pleasant face. He wore a red velvet cap on his shaved head in place of his large powdered wig.

"Remember, the Governor has set aside tomorrow as a Fast Day," Aunt Lydia told them both. "We'll go to Old South Church in the morning. Pastor Prince will pray for us to be saved from the French fleet."

The next day hundreds of people prayed at Old South. Johnny listened hard as the pastor said, "Send Thy tempest, Lord. Sink their proud ships with the power of Thy winds."

At that very moment the day darkened. Johnny could hardly see his aunt and uncle. High winds tore at the doors and windows of the church and shook the very building itself. The great church bell struck wildly once, twice—but no one was in the steeple to pull the bell. Everyone looked upward with astonishment and alarm.

"We hear thy voice, O Lord!" the parson cried out. It was an answer to their prayer, Johnny felt sure.

A week later several ships brought news that a terrible storm had sunk part of the French fleet. A fever had made ill or killed hundreds of French soldiers. Their admiral was dead. The fleet could no longer destroy the colonies.

All New England gave joyful thanks. "If God be for us, who can be against us?" everyone said.

Johnny was surer than ever that New England was a match for anyone.

# Chapter 5

# Johnny Saves a Sailor

Ten-year-old Johnny stretched his feet out toward the hot fire in Uncle Tom's library. He dropped his Greek textbook to the floor. Then he opened the new book, *Robinson Crusoe*, that Uncle Tom had given him just the night before.

"I must put my name in this," he said aloud. He found a quill pen in his uncle's desk.

He scratched out on the first page:

*John Hancock his book, November, 1747.*
*If this book I do lend and you do borrow,*
*Pray read it through today,*
*And send it home tomorrow.*

He smiled proudly as he looked at his writing. At last he could write a neat line, even though the letters were big.

Today was a school holiday. He was waiting for

Aunt Lydia's callers to leave. Then he and Aunt Lydia would drive to a shoemaker's shop on King Street. Johnny had outgrown his shoes.

Mrs. Edmund Quincy, who was Sam's aunt, had brought her newest baby to be admired. Six-month-old Dorothy Quincy was called "Dolly." Johnny could hear the ladies in the parlor.

"Huh! The way they're oohing and aahing over Dolly!" he snorted.

"Mistress is ready," young Cato came to tell him at last.

Aunt Lydia, in her large bonnet and warm red cloak, waited in the open carriage. Uncle Tom had ordered a fine yellow coach from England, but it had not come yet.

First, Aunt Lydia stopped at a dressmaker's shop. There the dressmaker showed her a new puppet, called a "fashion doll." It had just come from London and was dressed in the latest style in clothes.

The doll so pleased Aunt Lydia that dusk was coming by the time she reached the cobbler's shop. The shop faced Long Wharf.

The cobbler measured Johnny's feet for a pair of shoes with silver buckles and also for a pair of boots. While Aunt Lydia ordered her new shoes, Johnny peered out the shop window. He could see the lights of the British warships that were anchored out in the harbor.

Suddenly he saw eight or ten British sailors running up from Long Wharf. They all carried clubs. They caught three men walking along the waterfront, and dragged two of them back to the wharf and a waiting longboat.

The third man fought his way clear. He ran as fast as he could through the dusk. When he reached the cobbler's shop, he suddenly turned and darted in through the door. The little bell above the door jangled fiercely, "Ding-a-ling, ding!"

The shoemaker, Johnny, and Aunt Lydia all stared at the panting young man in seaman's clothes. A black eye and a bloody nose gave him a wild look. He had lost his knitted cap.

"Mercy!" exclaimed Aunt Lydia.

"Hide me!" cried the young man. "The King's sailors are sweeping the waterfront. They aim to fill their ships' crews. They'll be here looking for me in a moment!"

The cobbler found his tongue. "In here." He opened a door at the back of the shop. "Stay in this back room for a while and hide."

The young sailor croaked, "My thanks to ye, mate. Send warning. The British are taking landsmen as well as seamen."

With a quick nod to them all, he slipped through

the back door. Everything had happened so fast that Aunt Lydia hadn't found words. The cobbler gave her a worried look.

"I hope you are not angry with me, Madame Hancock," he said. "I couldn't let him be caught. He's an American seaman in our Boston fishing fleet. The British warships often try to kidnap our sailors. Life on those frigates is so bad the crews run off any chance they get. This is the start of a 'hot press,' I vow!"

Aunt Lydia's eyes shot sparks. "You did right. The idea! How wicked to beat men and take them aboard ships against their will! We must stop this business."

Johnny had heard talk of the impressment of American seamen before. This was the first time he had seen it happen. His face flushed with anger. He wished he were a grown man. He would go out and stop it!

"Come, Johnny. We must go home." Aunt Lydia moved toward the shop door.

"Wait, please, Auntie." Johnny caught her arm. An idea was growing in his mind. "Why can't we take that sailor with us in the carriage?"

"I don't know." Aunt Lydia frowned and thought a moment. Then to Johnny's relief she smiled and snapped, "We'll do it. A fine idea!"

"In here." He opened a door at the back of the shop.
"Stay in this back room for a while and hide."

Johnny ran outside to tell Prince. How quickly the waterfront had emptied! Somewhere out in the dimness covering the docks, he heard men's shouts and running feet.

Soon tall, stout Aunt Lydia hurried out to her carriage. Johnny walked on one side of her and Prince on the other. The young Boston sailor crept close behind them. He slipped up on the driver's seat next to Prince.

In a minute they were off at a fast trot through the empty streets. The soft glimmer of a house light here and there helped to show them the way home.

Back home, the sailor was hidden in the coach house until morning. Uncle Tom in his red velvet cap and blue dressing gown paced his study. He shook his head as Johnny and his aunt told about their adventure.

"It's that Captain Knowles! He's a hard man. He cares for nothing but the King's navy. He'll seize any man he finds, whether a seaman or a ship-builder's apprentice."

Aunt Lydia sat up straight in her brocaded chair. "We must not allow it. Do something!"

Uncle Tom slapped his hand on his desk. "I will, Madame. In the morning I shall call on the Governor. I'll insist that he must ask Captain Knowles to return the Americans he's taken aboard his warships. We have our rights!"

"Good for you, Uncle!" Johnny cried. He was proud of his Uncle Tom. "I wish I could hear you tell the Governor."

But Uncle Tom did not get to see the Governor. At midday, when Johnny came home from school for the dinner recess, his aunt told him Uncle Tom had sent her word.

"An angry crowd of dock workers, sailors, and the like gathered near the docks early this morning," she said. "They are armed with sticks, mops, and rusty swords. They've seized some British naval officers and threatened the Governor. The town's in an uproar. You must stay home from school this afternoon, Johnny."

Late that night Uncle Tom came back. "The members of the Governor's Council met in the Town House tonight," he said. "Several thousand people howled outside."

Johnny knew the Town House. It was the large government building at the head of King Street. Every year each town and village elected a man to sit in the General Assembly. These men met in the Town House.

"The Governor tried to calm the mob," Uncle Tom went on. "He hopes to get the kidnapped men back." He looked troubled. "We can't have mob rule.

Yet we are free Englishmen. We won't be treated as slaves."

The next day at school the boys talked excitedly about British Captain Knowles's threat to bombard the town if his officers were not freed. Several days later a town meeting of all the people was called.

The people of Boston agreed to return the navy officers to their ships. Captain Knowles took the kidnapped Boston men from the holds of his ships. He sent them ashore. Then he set sail. Boston was happy to see him go.

The Thanksgiving holidays came soon after this trouble. The Hancocks spent the day with Johnny's grandparents in Lexington. Then Johnny went on to Braintree to visit Jay Adams for several days.

Jay listened closely to Johnny's stories of the Boston riot.

"Won't King George be angry about the riot?" Jay asked thoughtfully.

"No," Johnny said, surprised. "It's not his fault. It's the Navy's."

The two boys climbed the hills of the North Common one day. Only a light powder of snow lay on the ground. On the way they talked about fishing through the ice. "How is Little Turtle?" Johnny asked suddenly. "Did you see him last summer? Do you still fish together?"

Jay grinned. "Aye, and he's not little. He's taller than you. He says he wants to be an army scout on our border. His uncle was a scout at the attack on Fort Louisburg."

Johnny gasped. "There was an Indian there with Sergeant Tim. He climbed into the Grand Battery and opened the gate. What if he were the same man? Wouldn't that be exciting?"

Jay shrugged and laughed. "Who knows? Maybe yes, maybe no. Race you to our gate!"

When Johnny left the next day, Jay promised to visit him during school holidays in August.

# Chapter 6

# Johnny Meets Sam Adams

Clark's wharf buzzed with action one August afternoon in 1748. Dock workers loaded army supplies on a Hancock ship.

"Phew!" Jay Adams, twelve, wrinkled his nose at the strong smell of tar and salt fish. This was the first day of his long-hoped-for visit with Johnny in Boston.

Johnny just leaned against a molasses barrel and laughed.

"So your uncle sends supplies to our men still holding Fort Louisburg?" Jay asked.

"Yes," replied Johnny. "The army orders are helping him to buy Clark's Wharf. What shall we do now? We've seen the sail loft and the ten shops here on the wharf. We've seen the kings and queens done in wax at the waxworks. We've still got some time before we meet Uncle Tom for supper at the Royal Tavern."

They dodged a carter pushing an empty cart.

"Go swimming?" Jay had his eyes on several boys. They had climbed the rigging of a near-by fishing boat and dived into the cool bay.

Johnny shook his head. "Aunt Lydia doesn't want me in the water, because I get sore throats and fever sometimes. It's silly, but she worries about me."

"Never mind," Jay told him cheerfully. "You will get to, someday. Let's walk over to the market hall in Dock Square. Fanueil Hall, you call it? That is, if we don't get run over by horses or knocked down by a carter."

They turned into a narrow crooked street known as Queen Street. A man coming from a shop was reading a small newspaper.

Jay looked at the paper and yelped. "Johnny! He's reading cousin Sam Adams' paper!"

"Your cousin's? How do you know?"

"I saw the words 'Independent Advertiser,' and there's a picture of a lady and a bird at the top of the page. I wonder—" Jay read the shop sign, "'Rogers and Fowles, Printers.' Maybe they would know about it. Let's go in."

"Why?" Johnny suddenly felt shy.

"Oh, come along." Jay stepped inside.

The empty room smelled musty. A counter and desk held some newspapers and books. The clumping noise of a printing press came through an open doorway from an inner room.

Johnny peeked through the doorway. He saw two men working at a wooden hand press. One turned the screw while the other pulled out each printed sheet as it was stamped. Light streamed from an open skylight above.

One of the men looked up. He came towards the boys, wiping his inky fingers on his leather apron. "What can I do for you young men?"

This made the boys laugh. "I'm looking for Sam Adams, a cousin of my father's," Jay told him. "I'm from Braintree. I hear that—"

The man turned. "Oh, Adams," he called.

For the first time, Johnny noticed a young man sitting at a table near the window. His quill pen raced over a long strip of foolscap. After a moment he laid down his pen and looked up from the page.

"What is it, Rogers?" he asked mildly.

Jay stepped around the press and bowed slightly to the young man. Sam Adams must be over twenty, Johnny decided. He wore no wig, just his plain brown hair. His clothes were not neat, or even clean.

Sam Adams seemed really pleased to meet the boys. "Father's read your paper," Jay said eagerly.

"That's how I knew it when I met that man outside. Father says you're the secret editor and that—"

Sam Adams waved his hand and smiled. "One can hear anything in Boston," he said. "I write a little for the paper, shall we say. Does he like the *Advertiser*?"

"We-e-ll—" Jay hesitated.

Sam Adams seemed really pleased to meet the boys

Sam shrugged. "I see. He thinks I'm too much in favor of the liberty of the colonies? Is that it, my boy?"

Jay looked puzzled. "I don't know about that, sir. He-he thinks you're against British rule and the King."

"Ah-h-h!" Sam pulled at his lower lip. "Not if King George gives us the rights of Englishmen. Do you know what liberty is, boys?"

"It's being free—" Johnny started to say.

"It's being free to help rule ourselves. Free to write and speak what we ourselves believe to be right. It's a gift from God. No one should force people against their wills. We are not England's slaves, whatever she thinks."

Johnny began to understand. "Aye! Like the British sailors kidnapping our Boston men. Our men didn't want to go aboard their ships. Neither the King nor our Governor said the sailors could take our men. So it was wrong for the Navy to kidnap them."

Sam Adams smiled pleasantly. "You learn fast. Do you plan to go to Cambridge to study at Harvard College?"

"Yes, sir, in two more years. I'll be thirteen then," Johnny said.

"And you, cousin John?" Adams turned to Jay.

Jay's blue eyes darkened. "If I ever learn enough Latin and Greek. I'd rather be a farmer."

"You'll get to college, I'm sure," Sam Adams told him. "Come to see me when you do. The river ferry costs only a penny. Now I must get back to my writing."

The boys left with a copy of the four-sheet newspaper. They promised not to say they had seen

Adams at the printer's shop.

The next day Sam and Ned Quincy came to see Johnny and Jay. They found the boys in the stables, brushing Imp and the colt that Johnny had ridden up from Braintree.

"Guess what's happened!" the Quincy boys said excitedly. "We bet you can't guess."

"You found a three-legged cat, or a bag of gold." Johnny grinned at them.

"That's right! What luck! You'd never believe it!" Sam said.

"Which is it?" Jay laughed.

"Gold, simple! You know the *Bethel,* the ship Father and Uncle Ed Quincy own? Well, it captured a Spanish treasure ship, the *Jesu Maria,* with a cargo of silver and gold. We're rich!"

"How did it happen? How could such a small ship capture a big Spanish ship?"

"I'll tell it. I'm the oldest," Ned said to Sam. "The *Bethel* was going through the Straits of Gibraltar at dusk. Suddenly it saw the *Jesu Maria's* lights. The *Bethel* was too small to get away. So guess what our captain did?"

"What?" Johnny was wide-eyed.

"He hung lanterns high in the rigging. The crew fixed sticks with hats and coats on them to look like men. They set these along the rails. Then our captain bore down full sail on the *Jesu Maria* and demanded that it surrender."

"And he fooled the Spanish?"

Ned smiled. "Yes, in the dusk the Spanish captain thought our ship was a British war sloop. He surrendered without a shot."

"It's hard to believe, but wonderful!" Johnny said. "How many men did the Spanish have?"

"One hundred and ten men and twenty-six guns. And the *Bethel* had only thirty-seven men and fourteen guns," Sam said proudly. He was about ready to burst.

Johnny gave Imp a slap on the flank with his brush. "First the French and now the Spanish," he said. "I tell you, New England men can beat anybody!" He chuckled happily.

"Father and Uncle Ed might sell their shipbuilding business," Sam went on. "They want to move back to Braintree."

"I'd hate to see you go. We'd miss you at school and all—"

"Oh, we don't know how soon," Sam replied easily. "We'll finish school here, I think. I'll follow Ned to college at Cambridge. That is, if I pass the entrance examinations."

The boys all rolled their eyes. They'd already learned that the examinations required answering questions in Latin and Greek.

All too soon Jay's week in Boston passed. He had to return home to school. The three weeks in August were the only summer vacation the boys had.

Jay had ridden his colt up to town with a neighbor who had brought in a load of vegetables. Although Uncle Tom didn't like it, Jay insisted on riding the ten miles back alone.

"I'm almost thirteen," he exclaimed. "I'm old enough to find my way home."

The coachman fastened Jay's box behind his saddle. The saddle bags were stuffed with gifts for his family from the Hancocks. Prince and Johnny rode with him as far as the city gates.

Jay gave a last wave and trotted off.

Johnny put his fingers to his mouth and whistled shrilly. "Greet Little Turtle for me if you see him fishing."

# Chapter 7

# Snowballs and Paul Revere

One afternoon late in the year 1748, Uncle Thomas stamped into his front hall. He dropped his news-sheet, the *Independent Advertiser,* on a marble table.

Johnny came down the curved stairway for tea.

"Lydia!" Uncle Tom shouted. "And you, Johnny! Come into the library." His double chins shook. Johnny had never seen him so angry.

Uncle Tom limped ahead. Johnny could tell that his gout hurt him.

Uncle Tom sat down slowly with a groan. "We have had bad news today," he said. "England has returned Fort Louisburg in Canada to France! The treaty was signed in October. That's the thanks our heroes get for their capture of the gateway to the St. Lawrence River! It's all for nothing!"

Johnny and Aunt Lydia gasped.

Aunt Lydia said sadly, "It's a shame! How dare they? Is there nothing we can do?"

"Humph!" Uncle Tom snorted. "There's nothing we can do. It's done. But New England won't forget this. All our merchants are furious!"

"Tim O'Toole won't like it. Neither will any of the militia," Johnny spoke up.

"The militia say they won't fight for England again," Uncle Tom went on. "They're that angry. And why shouldn't they be? A treaty won't keep the French or their Indian allies from killing our western settlers."

Uncle Tom held up the little *Independent Advertiser.* "Here's one news-sheet that's not afraid to speak up," he said. "You must both read it. The editor reminds England that our country, our Massachusetts, has lost seven thousand men, sick or dead. Many farms have gone to ruin. As a landowner, I know that well!"

"Are you ready for tea?" Aunt Lydia reached for a silver bell.

"No! This writer even says that England doesn't care about us—that we should cut our ties with her. Hmmm. I wonder who dared to write this?"

"People say the names of the writers for that paper are kept secret," Aunt Lydia said.

Johnny felt a secret thrill of pleasure. He thought, "Sam Adams wrote that. At least someone dares to let England know what we think."

Near the end of December high snow drifts lined the streets. They filled the narrow lanes. The drifts were piled higher by the plows used to clear the streets. Harness bells jingled merrily as horses trotted along the streets pulling covered sleighs.

"Take this note over to Colonel Josiah Quincy's for me, Johnny," his aunt said one Saturday afternoon after school.

"Yes, ma'am." Johnny was pleased. He wanted to see Sam.

Soon he was on his way. His boots squeaked over the packed snow. He buried his mouth in the knitted scarf his mother had sent him.

Two older boys came down the street towards him. They wore gray greatcoats, knit caps, and leather breeches. The bigger one carried a basket under his arm. They were laughing.

As they hurried past him, Johnny had a quick look in the basket. It was filled with snowballs!

"So!" Johnny thought. He turned his head. "The boys are gone. They must have slipped into that narrow lane I just passed."

He picked up some snow in his mittened hands and made a snowball. As he straightened up something whizzed past his head. Wham! Another snowball smacked against his back. He whirled around, but he could see no one.

Close by snow had drifted high against the front of a house. Johnny ran and dropped behind it. He waited.

Soon two heads peeked out of the lane. Then the two boys ran out to the street to look for their target.

Johnny jumped up. As fast as he could, he threw two snowballs. One missed, but the other hit the bigger boy full in the face. With a yell he slipped and fell to the street. Snowballs rolled from his basket.

Quick as a wink, Johnny ran back to the smaller boy, who was trying to pick up the snowballs. Johnny scooped up a chunk of snow and threw it over the boy's head.

"O-h-h, you—" the boy roared and grabbed at Johnny. Johnny dodged away. At that moment the bigger boy got to his feet.

"I've seen him before," Johnny thought. "Now what's his name?"

The smaller boy took a step forward. He was grinning and wiping the snow from his face. "Let's get him, Paul."

Paul laughed. "We've met our match, Joe. And I know you," he said to Johnny. "You're the lucky fellow who lives in the grand house on Beacon Hill yonder. Your uncle comes to my father's shop. I'm Paul Revere and this is Joe."

As fast as he could, he threw two snowballs. One missed,
but the other hit the bigger boy full in the face.

Johnny smiled. "I thought I knew you. Do you still live near Clark's Wharf?"

"Aye, we do. I'm through North Writing School and learning to be a silversmith. I just left a copper teakettle at a house down the street." Paul grinned. "And I don't like an empty basket," he added.

So that was why Johnny hadn't seen more of Paul Revere. The Reading and Writing Schools were for boys who would not go on to Harvard College but would become tradesmen. Many boys didn't even go to the Writing Schools.

Joe poked Paul. "Come on. We'll be late for bell practice at Old North."

"Old North" was what everyone in Boston called Christ's Church. Christ's Church was not a New England or Puritan church but an Episcopal or English church. It had a "royal peal" of bells that were said to be the sweetest and best bells in America. They could be heard in Cambridge clear across the Charles River.

"We've a club of bell-ringers," Paul told Johnny. "Seven of us are paid for ringing the bells on Sundays and at other times, too. Since Christmas is day after tomorrow, we have to go over and practice now."

Christmas! Johnny was curious. The Puritans had thought it wicked to celebrate Christmas, and many New Englanders still thought so. Most of them, like Johnny's family, celebrated New Year's instead, with a school holiday and little gifts.

Johnny had heard how beautiful the Episcopal churches looked at Christmas. "I'd like to see Old North and hear you boys," he said. "Will you let me come, too?"

"Aye, come along. But it's a far walk."

When Paul and Joe pushed open the big doors of Christ's Church the wonderful smell of Christmas evergreens was everywhere.

Johnny looked at the church's carved altar, at which candles were burning. He looked at the organ and the carved wooden statues, and his eyes grew wide. "How beautiful it is! So different from our plain church!" he said.

He saw several boys, their faces red from cold, hustle into the bell-tower. Paul followed them. Soon Johnny could hear the bell-ringer telling the boys how to ring a Christmas carol. When the music started, Johnny thought he could feel the ringing clear to his bones.

The New England Sabbath began at candle-lighting time on Saturday. So Johnny soon had to leave. Paul was still up in the bell-tower pulling hard at the bell ropes, but Johnny felt that he had made a new friend.

# Chapter 8

# Johnny Gets a Degree and Loses Two Friends

The day was damp and misty. Johnny rode through the countryside with Aunt Lydia in their new yellow coach.

They were on their way to Cambridge and Harvard College. Johnny was thirteen and ready to take his entrance examinations there.

It would have been shorter to go by ferry across the Charles River. But the flat raft used as a ferry was unsafe for Aunt Lydia and the big coach.

Johnny shifted uneasily on the scarlet cushions. How he wished Uncle Tom hadn't been kept at home with his gout!

"What will the other fellows think," he wondered, "of my coming to the college with a coach and an aunt?"

He sighed. "If only Sam Quincy could have come today instead of tomorrow!"

He scratched his head. His wig itched. Now that he was soon to be in college, Aunt Lydia said he had to wear a wig.

"Don't fidget so!" Aunt Lydia said.

"Yes, ma'am." He had been told what to expect today by Ned Quincy, who was already going to college. Four tutors and President Holyoke of Harvard would ask him questions. The questions would be in Latin and he must answer in Latin. Then he must change English into Latin and Greek.

He had his head out the open window as the coach neared Cambridge Common. The College faced the Common. A fence enclosed the College's three long brick buildings, which surrounded a square of land called the "yard." This yard was bare except for a large elm tree.

The coach stopped in front of a building. "Here's Harvard Hall, where I'm to report, Auntie," Johnny said.

"I'll rest at the inn," Aunt Lydia said. "Don't fret. You'll do well, John."

Johnny gave her a smile, although he felt shaky inside. "Yes, ma'am, I'll try."

He went in alone. About fifteen boys were sitting on benches, awaiting their turns. Some looked very young and frightened. Others tried not to look uneasy. They seemed to be from twelve to eighteen years of age.

When his turn came, Johnny walked into a room paneled in wood. The President stood by a desk, wearing a black silk gown and a white bib collar. He bowed and so did Johnny.

"Ah! It's-ah-John Hancock?" He looked at the list on his desk. "I know your uncle. He's been most kind to our college."

"Yes, sir." Johnny let out his breath.

Then two teachers in black gowns and white wigs stepped forward and began to ask questions in Latin. Finally one of them gave Johnny a paper written in English. "Change this into Latin. You may use the study next door."

Johnny didn't learn how well he did in his work, but he was told later to make a copy of the college laws. Then he was told to bring his copy of the laws with him in August and he would be entered as a freshman.

Aunt Lydia was delighted. "I knew you could do it! Now we must return to Boston at once. If your uncle's gout improves, we shall come back for Commencement Day next week. Would you like that, John?"

"Wonderful!" Johnny said. "Aunt Lydia, I feel so much better, now that it's over. I could dance a jig!"

The Hancocks almost always came to Cambridge

for Commencement Day. That was the day on which seniors were graduated from college. Held the second week in July, it was the biggest holiday in Massachusetts. Everyone in the colony was proud of Harvard College.

Uncle Thomas was well enough to go to Cambridge the next week. The Hancocks came in their best satins and brocades. Uncle Tom sported gold buttons and gold shoe buckles. Aunt Lydia's hoop skirt was so large that Johnny and his uncle barely could squeeze into the big yellow coach.

At eleven o'clock Johnny stood outside the Meeting House. He felt warm in his peach-colored satin coat and blue satin breeches.

The church bell began to ring. Then he heard fifes and music. "Here they come!" people gathered before the church murmured.

Johnny watched in awe as all the students marched into the church. After them came President Holyoke, then the Royal Governor and other important people. All were dressed in bright silks and velvets or red and gold uniforms.

"You and your uncle have been given front row seats," Aunt Lydia whispered as she and Johnny and Uncle Tom pushed through the crowd into the church.

Uncle Thomas was well enough to go to Cambridge
the next week. The Hancocks came in their best
satins and brocades.

Johnny could see that she was pleased. She went happily upstairs to sit with the other ladies in the balcony.

After many speeches, the black-robed seniors were given their bachelor of arts degrees. "Will I ever learn enough to win one, too?" Johnny wondered.

He glanced back at Sam Quincy, who sat in the row behind him. Sam looked back solemnly, and then slowly winked.

Johnny almost giggled. "If Sam isn't worried, why should I be?" He sat back and waited for the end of the program. Then he could enjoy the acrobats and dancing on the Common and the dinner that would follow.

"Another month and I'll be part of all this!" he thought.

"Freshman Hancock! Oh, Hancock!" Thirteen-year-old Johnny felt someone shaking him.

"What? What?" He sat up in his narrow bed and rubbed his eyes.

A Harvard sophomore, a second-year man, stood over him. He wore a black gown with a plaid lining and held a fuzzy wig in his hands. "Take this over to the barber's to be curled before breakfast," he ordered.

"Before breakfast?" Johnny was dismayed. That meant he wouldn't have time to eat at the Buttery. All the college students snatched a bite of biscuit and milk there. "Yes, sir," he groaned. He watched the sophomore strut out of the room with a pleased smile.

Johnny was a new Harvard student. He was bound not only by the school rules but also by the class rules. A freshman had to obey every upper classman.

His day started with church at six in the morning. At 6:30 he went to his first class. After that came breakfast, then more classes.

He ate dinner in the "Commons," a large eating hall. He washed his meat and vegetables down with cider. The cider was passed from person to person in two huge pewter mugs, which were scoured only once a week.

His afternoons from two o'clock until supper Johnny spent in study. After a supper of meat pie or bread and milk, he studied in his room.

"This isn't the exciting life I'd thought it would be," Johnny said to Sam Quincy as they settled down for an evening's reading.

In December of that year he was called to Lexington, for Grandfather Hancock had suddenly died. Johnny hired a horse at the stables and galloped over the snow-covered roads.

At the parsonage he greeted his family. His mother had come with her husband, Parson Daniel Perkins. Sister Mary was there, too, and schoolboy Ebenezer. Parson Perkins's son, Richard, had eyes for no one but sister Mary.

"How tall you've grown this past year," Mother said. She patted Johnny proudly.

"So handsome, too," Mary teased.

Johnny stood up and made a deep bow. "Thank you, ladies," he said jokingly, but his thin cheeks turned red.

"John is a good student at Harvard," Uncle Tom said proudly. "He will be a help to me in my business."

After the funeral Johnny returned to school. For the next two years he continued to study Latin, Greek, religion, and famous English writers. In his fourth and last year he studied arithmetic, geometry, and geography.

Just before he finished college his sister Mary married Richard Perkins. Then all the family came to Cambridge on July 17, 1754, to enjoy Johnny's graduation. He was seventeen.

Uncle Tom took Johnny into his business at once as a clerk. He had a desk by a window looking out on the docks. Around the corner was the noisy market square.

"Rattle, thump, rum-te-tum!" Johnny muttered as he dipped his quill pen into his inkhorn one day. "How can anyone think?"

He was making copies of all the business orders which Uncle Tom sent to England and Europe. These copies were kept in a "letter book." Often several copies of a letter were sent on different ships. Sometimes ships were lost or captured during a war.

"Whatever became of your clerk, Tim O'Toole?" Johnny asked his uncle one day. "I thought he was your best clerk."

"Aye, so he was. But he wanted to start his own shop, so I helped him to do it. He's getting along fine, too."

"I'm glad to hear it. I must call on him. You were always good about helping young men in business, Uncle Tom."

During the next few years Johnny worked hard to learn the vast Hancock business. Uncle Tom had spells of gout, and the work fell more and more on Johnny's shoulders.

War with France was brewing again, for France wanted the Ohio River country. Uncle Tom got orders to supply the British troops in the colonies. His ships began to collect army supplies from England and various places along the coast. Soon England declared war on France.

"It's an honor to meet you, Major," nineteen-year-old
Johnny said with a bow.

One night Uncle Tom brought home a young
army officer from Virginia. He was taller than
Johnny and had merry blue eyes and powdered,
reddish hair.

"This is Major George Washington," Uncle Tom
said. "He fought with General Braddock out in the
Ohio country."

"It's an honor to meet you, Major," nineteen-
year-old Johnny said with a bow. He felt honored

indeed. Major Washington had had two horses shot from under him during the fight. If it had not been for him, Braddock's defeat by the French and Indians would have been even worse.

The young Major told Johnny that he had come to talk to the Massachusetts Governor about fighting the French. "The British must learn to fight from behind trees as the Indians do," he said. "Then we can win."

"Heh, I'll see that the Governor heeds that advice, young man," Uncle Tom said with a nod. "We have to protect our settlers, and we must take Fort Louisburg again."

Two years later, in 1758, Fort Louisburg was recaptured. Then, on a bright September day, General Amherst and his four thousand troops returned to Boston and camped on the Common. All Boston welcomed them.

"This time we'll keep Fort Louisburg," everyone said happily. "The St. Lawrence River is open. France's power in America is broken."

The next morning Johnny came down the stone steps of his house. He heard drums and fifes sounding briskly over the Common.

"I want to go to the British Coffee House for dinner this noon," he told Uncle Tom. "I'd like to hear firsthand about the capture of Louisburg. Surely some of the officers will be there today."

"Aye, John, go along," Uncle Tom said. "I have government business at the Town House. Be sure to ask after Lieutenant Tim O'Toole."

That noon Johnny sat at a table in the crowded inn and talked to several young officers. "Didn't you know Lieutenant Timothy O'Toole?" he said to one officer he knew.

The young man looked sad. "Yes, I knew him. He was killed, I'm sorry to say."

"Killed!" Johnny was shocked. He wet his lips and swallowed hard. "This is terrible news. I knew him a long time ago."

"He went out with a patrol of scouts. There was an Indian along by the name of Little Turtle. They were caught by a French patrol, but they gave warning in time for the rest of our patrol to escape."

"Little Turtle, too!" Johnny shook his head. How odd that two friends from childhood should die together! His eyes grew dim and he pushed away his pewter plate.

"If only England hadn't been so stupid and given Fort Louisburg back to the French that first time!" he said bitterly. "My friends might not have had to die now."

The British officers frowned, but Johnny didn't care. He didn't even notice them.

# Chapter 9

# Merchant and Signer for Independence

John continued to work in his uncle's business. He helped to expand it by overseeing the building of three fast ships to carry their goods to and from England.

When his uncle died, John became the richest man in New England and the second richest in America. His uncle left him about 80,000 pounds in English money.

John soon became part of the group of colonists protesting a new tax on American business. Called the Stamp Act, it required that every piece of business paper and newspaper must have a tax stamp on it. They succeeded in getting the act repealed— only to learn that a new tax would replace it.

When John refused to pay the new tax, one of his ships was seized by the British. He won his case,

One evening more than 150 Bostonians, dressed in blankets with soot-blackened faces, rowed out into the harbor, climbed aboard the ships and dumped the entire cargo of tea into the sea.

but didn't get his ship back.

Several years later, England thought of a new plan to raise taxes and to get rid of her tea at the same time. Once more Americans rose up in arms. On every side John heard people say, "We'll neither buy nor drink the tea. We will not be taxed without our consent."

In December, 1773, three British ships, the *Dartmouth,* the *Beaver,* and the *Eleanor,* reached Boston. Each ship contained 114 chests of tea that carried the hated tax. The people of Boston would not buy the tea or let it land. The English Governor Hutchinson would not permit the ships to leave the harbor.

One evening more than 150 Bostonians, dressed in blankets with soot-blackened faces, rowed out into the harbor, climbed aboard the ships and dumped the entire cargo of tea into the sea.

The British closed the port of Boston, and filled the town with troops. John learned of secret orders to arrest him and Sam Adams for treason.

John left for Concord, planning to stay at the Clark-Hancock parsonage, and then travel on to Philadelphia to be a delegate in the Second Continental Congress.

At midnight on April 18 a horseman galloped past Lexington Green. He sped up Bedford Turnpike to the Clark-Hancock parsonage.

A group of Minute Men stood guard around the frame house. They called out, "Halt!"

John, resting upstairs, heard the rider cry, "I want to see John Hancock and Sam Adams."

"Not so much noise," said Sergeant Will Monroe. "You'll awaken the whole family."

"Noise!" said the rider. "You'll have noise enough before long. The Regulars are coming!"

Windows were raised. Both Parson Clark and John stuck their heads out.

John saw Paul Revere standing in the cold moonlight. "Come in, Revere. We are not afraid of you," he said.

Quickly Paul Revere gave his message. "Dr. Warren sent me and Will Dawes to warn you and all the countryside," he said. "The British Regulars are marching from Boston. They are to arrest you and Sam Adams and capture our store of powder and supplies at Concord."

"We must leave at once," Sam Adams said.

John went to the door in his silk dressing gown. "Ring the church bell for the alarm," he told the Minute Men.

John saw Paul Revere standing in the cold moonlight.

John began to clean his sword and pistol. He was determined to stay and fight the British.

Soon Will Dawes arrived. The two messengers had something to eat, then rode off toward Concord to spread the alarm.

Later in the night a tired Paul Revere stumbled into the parsonage. "I was captured by several British officers," he reported. "They took my good horse. After a while they let me go, just outside this village. I walked back. Will Dawes escaped and went on."

By now it was almost dawn. The church bell was still ringing, *ding, dong, dong.* The rattle and roll of a drum brought the militia to the Green. Word came that six companies of British Regulars were almost at hand.

Finally John put on his scarlet cloak. He climbed into his carriage along with Sam and Paul. "If I had my musket, I would never turn my back on these troops," he said.

They drove to a house only two miles away in Woburn village. Then John sent Paul back to Lexington. "I've left a leather trunk at Buckman's Tavern," he said. "Do you think you can get it? It's full of important papers for our Provincial Congress and must not be lost."

Later John learned that Paul carried the trunk through the seventy-seven farmers drawn up on the

Green. Just after Paul had reached the road he heard the first shots of the Revolution.

John heard the distant shots, too. "It's begun," he said. "I wonder what's happening."

He and Sam Adams moved from place to place to hide from the British soldiers. Then they started south to the Continental Congress at Philadelphia. All along the way, they and other delegates were led into the towns by large crowds of people and companies of militia.

Philadelphia was the largest and richest town in America. John looked with interest at its neat brick houses and tree-lined streets.

The first day he walked to the State House on Chestnut Street with John Adams and the other delegates. Old friends greeted one another in a beautiful, white-paneled room with two large fireplaces.

Ben Franklin arrived in his brown Quaker coat. George Washington came from Virginia in an elegant blue and buff uniform and a sword. Soon he would be offered the command of the thousands of militia that had gathered outside the city of Boston.

"Let us make John Hancock President of Congress," the delegates said to one another. "He was one of the first to oppose King George. He's a great leader. Without his help the Boston patriots could not have held out."

John was surprised and pleased. His friend Benjamin Harrison of Virginia placed him in the President's chair. "We will show Britain how much we think of her making you an outlaw," he said heartily.

At once John was swallowed up in work. As the leader of Congress he had to plan a war. He begged supplies from the colonies. They were jealous of one another and slow to send men or money. John's pen was busy scratching out orders and letters.

The British troops held Boston. Congress talked about burning the town to drive them away. John owned many houses there, but he wrote to General Washington: "If you must burn Boston, I heartily wish it. Even though I may suffer the greatest loss."

He was deep in planning a navy, too. Congress ordered thirteen ships to be built and made John chairman of the Marine Committee.

Still more letters flowed from John's pen. He urged all colonists to change merchant ships into warships. Massachusetts built two war frigates, the *Hancock* and the *Boston.*

One day in March, 1776, an express rider brought a letter to John from General Washington. "The British have left Boston!" the General wrote.

It was an American victory.

The afternoon of Thursday, July 4, 1776, was hot. The tired delegates of the Continental Congress gathered in the State House in Philadelphia stopped talking. Some of them moved closer to John Hancock, who was standing at a mahogany table in the front of the room. They held their breaths and watched. For John was reading a hand-written paper lying on the table.

"Will he dare sign the paper alone?" one delegate whispered to another. "If the Revolution fails, he'll be called a traitor. England will hang him, surely."

"He's a brave man," the other delegate replied. "He'll sign. Anyhow, he's already been called a traitor and threatened with hanging."

John drew a pen from the silver inkstand on the table. Then, leaning forward, he signed his name in a beautiful hand.

John drew a pen from the silver inkstand on the table.
Then, leaning forward, he signed his name in a
beautiful hand.

"It's done!" he said aloud. "As President of
Congress, I have signed America's Declaration of
Independence from England!"

Then he added, "We shall have this printed right
away. This Declaration will be sent to our armies
and to every town in America."

A few days later he stood in the State House yard. He heard the Declaration read to the public for the first time.

"Huzzah for the United States! Huzzah for Congress and John Hancock! Now we are free!" the crowd shouted.

John's heart swelled with pride. "But we still have to fight hard for that freedom," he told the crowd. "We must never give up."

All the new states celebrated the joyful news. They had parades and burned bonfires.

John's name was the only one on the first printed copy of the Declaration. Congress ordered a beautiful parchment copy to be made.

On this parchment fifty members of Congress signed their names on August 2. Again John signed first in his large, bold hand.

"There!" he said. He handed the quill to the next delegate. "England can read my name without glasses. She may now double her reward for my head."

In the years to come, John Hancock continued to work to hold Congress together and to win the war for independence. He became the first governor of the state of Massachusetts, and helped to create the Constitution and the Bill of Rights. But it is for his big, bold signature on the Declaration of Independence that he is best remembered.

# What Happened Next?

• John Hancock had two children a daughter, Lydia, and a son, John George Washington. Both of them died at a young age.

• John Hancock retired from the Continental Congress in 1777 due to illness, but was elected the first Governor of Massachusetts in 1780.

• In the presidential election of 1789, Hancock won 4 electoral votes.

• He was reelected as Massachusetts governor nine times and served until his death in 1793.

# When John Hancock Lived

| Date | Event |
|------|-------|
| 1737 | John Hancock was born in Braintree, Massachusetts on January 23. There were 13 English colonies in America ruled by King George II. |
| 1750–1764 | John Hancock went to Harvard and worked. |
| 1754–1763 | The French and Indian War began and ended. |
| 1764–1775 | John inherited and operated his uncle's business. |
| 1773 | The Boston Tea Party took place. |
| 1775 | The first battle of the Revolutionary War was fought at Lexington, Massachusetts. |
| 1775–1777 | John Hancock was President of the Second Continental Congress. |
| 1776 | John Hancock signed the Declaration of Independence. |

1777–1783   John became a political leader and Governor of Massachusetts.

1783        Peace treaty with England was signed, ending the Revolutionary War.

1787        The Constitutional Convention met to frame the Constitution the United States.

1793        John Hancock died on October 8. There were 13 states in the Union. George Washington was President.

# Fun Facts About
# John Hancock

• John Hancock was the first and only signer of the Declaration of Independence on July 4, 1776. The rest of the delegates signed several weeks later.

• Hancock's signature was so large that to this day, the slang expression for your "signature" is "your John Hancock."

• A life insurance company and six United States Navy ships have been named for John Hancock.

• Mr. Hancock founded a school for boys called the Adams Academy. It is now a museum located on the site of John's birthplace in Braintree (now Quincy), Massachusetts.

Visit www.patriapress.com/hancock to learn more about John Hancock.

# What Does That Mean?

**foolscap**—sheets of writing paper.

**counting-room**—The room where businessmen kept track of their money and papers.

**pell-mell**—in a confused rush.

**New England primer**—an early school book used to teach children to read.

**frigate**—a medium-sized warship.

**Huzzah**—Hurray!

**quill**—pen made from a bird's feather.

# About the Author

"My message is love of country and I think we ought to appreciate what we've got," observed Kathryn Sisson. "No country on earth has what we have." Newspaper reporter, publicist and author of numerous articles and books, Mrs. Sisson was a lifelong member and Vice Regent of the Boca Raton chapter of the Daughters of the American Revolution. She served as a vice president of the National League of American Penwomen, and was a member of the Women's National Book Association, Society of Midland Authors and the Children's Reading Round Table of Chicago. Children's books penned in addition to *John Hancock, Independent Boy* include *Eddie Rickenbacker, Boy Pilot and Racer; Black Hawk, Young Sauk Warrior* and *Famous American Patriots for Young People,* which earned Mrs. Sisson the Dolly Madison Award from the Sons of the American Revolution.